Greenwich

For Petronella Breinburg

First published in 2021
By Hikari Press, London

www.hikaripress.co.uk

Distributed in the UK by
Combined Book Services Limited
Paddock Wood Distribution Centre
Paddock Wood
Tonbridge
Kent TN12 6UU

www.combook.co.uk

ISBN: 978-0-9956478-9-3

British Library Cataloguing-in-Publication-Data.
A catalogue record of the book is available from the British Library.

Designed by Dani Leigh Design
www.danileighdesign.com
and printed in the UK by Gomer Press
www.gomerprinting.co.uk

Sadie and the Sea Dogs

written by Maureen Duffy

illustrated by Anita Joice

HIKARI
PRESS

To put to sea and voyage far away
Through ice-green waters where the great whales play

Was Sadie's dream. She lived beside the Thames

At Greenwich where the water bus route ends

And in the evenings after tea was done
She'd stand and watch against the sun
Black shapes of barges surging by
And long to Stow away or be a cabin boy.

'Dreamer,' Mum called her. 'Always miles away.

Why don't you go with Linda out to play?'

Linda liked skipping or running with a ball,

Hopscotch or jacks and handstands up the wall.

'You've never been the same,' her mother said,

'Since that museum went and filled your head

With admirals, and ships and sailors dead

And gone for donkey's years.' And it was true,

At home or school, whatever she had to do,

She thought of them, on errands, and washing-up too.

Her class had gone one rainy afternoon
When all the houses cowered in the gloom,
To the Maritime Museum...

And there inside
she'd found a different world

NATIONAL MARITIME MUSEUM

Where rigging sang
and white winged sails unfurled.

O ne day when she got home,
May, her country aunt

Had come to tea. 'I know just what you want;

Fresh air. You're looking pale. You come and stay

With us a while. Now what d'you say?

The change will do you good. That's settled then.

Come down as soon as holidays begin.'

S adie was desolate. What could she do?
To leave the river and her dreaming too.

Term ended. There was one day more.

She wandered for the last time through the door.

P ast the brass cannon, and at once her ears
    Were filled with gulls' cries. Like salt spray the tears
Sharp stung her eyes. She crept into a corner there
And curled up small beneath a glass case where
Nelson's Trafalgar breeches are on show.
She fell asleep. The shadows longer grow.

She doesn't hear the bell calling out,
Nor the attendant's warning shout.

Until cramp and her strange bed woke her, or the sound

Of angry voices. She started, peered around.

Where was she? And then she knew. What should she do?

Her Mum would be so wild, and worried too.

And then she saw a light beneath a door

And heard behind a kind of muted roar

Like stormy seas. She tiptoed close to hear

Voices upraised. 'We go tonight, all clear?

Our shipmates down the road are ready now.

No time to lose. All follow me. Let's go.'

The door swung open. She'd no place to hide.

'What have we here? Bosun, bring her inside.'

Fierce faces stared at her on either hand,

    Stiff painted shapes that seemed to stand

As if their limbs were carved from wood,

And their strange clothes. Then Sadie understood.

'The figureheads!'

'That's right.' Their leader smiled.

'I'm Arethusa. What's your name, my child?'

'Sadie.' 'Right, Sadie, you must come along

With us.' Around her now the strange shapes throng.

'I should be going home.' 'Too late for that.'

The eyes grow stern. One in a tricorne hat

Cries, 'Yardarm or plank,

    you can take your choice

Or sail with us.' Each adds their voice.

15

So Sadie goes along a sleeping street
That echoes to their clattering wooden feet
But no one hears. No window opens wide
To see them marching to the riverside

Where a tall ship

was rocking on the tide.

The Cutty Sark: Sadie knew it well
But out of drydock now with sails that swell
And billow in the evening breeze. 'Let go aft!'
Cries Arethusa and the eager crew cast
Off the ropes. The Isle of Dogs slips past
And Sadie's sailing down the Thames at last.

She watches as her own home slides away.

If she could see her now what would her mother say?

Bosun was Boadicea, first mate was Hood.
The crew all knew their posts. The wind was good,
The ebb tide drew them quickly down

And soon they'd sailed beyond the town.

The captain says, 'Break out the grog,

Mister Hood.' 'Aye aye Capn.' 'Fetch me the log.'

'Excuse me,' Sadie asked, 'where are we bound?'

'The wide Atlantic, beyond Plymouth Sound.'

'No time for questions now. Able seamen,

Instruct this new cabin-boy as best you can.'

A figurehead saluted, then with a wink

To Sadie said, 'Best come below, I think.'

'I'm Ajax.' He wore a helmet, breastplate and kilt.

'I don't suppose you've heard but once we built...'

'A wooden horse,' said Sadie. 'You were at Troy,

A Greek.' He sighed, 'When I was just a boy,

And see me now: a conquering king become

On this trip nothing but an able seaman.'

'I'm sorry,' Sadie said. Ajax replied: 'Enough of that.

Why should I quarrel even if I'm just ship's cat.

A ship's a country; follow what I mean?

It needs us all. Our captain's brave and keen.

She knows her job. I'll sail with her.' 'But where?'

Sadie says then. 'And why? What're you doing here?'

'We're off to sink the national debt with gold.

Tortuga's stuffed with treasure, so we're told.'

pieces of eight

'There's galleons long foundered where the fish

Wear pearly crowns, and when King Neptune dines each dish

Is set with rubies. There's such a store

Of necklaces as even Queen Helen never wore.

You see the mermaid there with tail tucked in?

She'll raise the treasure chests.

    You know how they can swim.'

'And then?' asked Sadie. 'We'll bring it safe and sound

Back home to London to prop up the pound.'

'But why?' said Sadie. 'Why not sail away

And live a roving life?' 'That's the pirate's way,'

Said Ajax, 'We're navy, merchant and royal;

To hear you talk of pirates makes me boil.

We're bound to meet some on this trip, don't fear.

You'll find them very different when you see them near,

Not the romantic lot you thought before.

They hardly know a capstan from an oar.'

22

'It's nearly morning. The dawn begins to break,
And look the flying fishes are awake
Starting to sail alongside. How she skims too,
Our graceful clipper.' Like a gull she flew.
While all the world went racing past until
A rainbow like a bubble wrapped her round;
So fast she goes she never makes a sound
But slips through seas like a hot knife through butter;
So stiff her pennants stand they hardly flutter.

The sun climbs up and up but she runs on
Till 'Land ahoy!' the lookout cries at noon.

She slows and now at last Sadie can hear

The ropes and masts and water music clear,

And then the anchor-chain clanks overboard.

It's crystal clear down there where they are moored.

The brilliant fishes dash about below

Flirting their tails. Like gems themselves they glow.

'And now, Sabrina dear, call up your chums,'
Says Arethusa. The mermaid whistles through her thumbs.

In a trice the glass waves swirled

About the ship. The mermaid blew some sweet sharp notes.

The dolphins answered from their own deep throats.
How Sadie longed to know their language too.

25

The mermaid and her friends dived down from view
Deep, deep beneath the ship while all the crew
Leant on the rails. The water boils again.

Two dolphins heave a heavy chest between them

And toss it on the poop. 'Let go the net,'
The captain calls. It comes up dripping wet
And bulging. Sabrina riding on the rope
Waves. The dolphins in a chorus bob and dip.

'Don't go,' cries Sadie, leaning out too far.

She topples over like a falling star
  Or that boy who flew too near the burning sun

Till his waxed feathers were all undone

And down he fell. So Sadie tumbles too.

Quicker than thought one dolphin threw

A double somersault and jack-knifes down

Below her, afraid that she might drown,

And raises her over the foaming spray
  To safety. She sees the strong muscles grey

Ripple beneath her and puts her arms where

She can hold. Sadie whispered in his ear,

'Thank you.' Though she'd learnt to swim at Greenwich baths

She'd never ridden dolphin back along the ocean paths.

The crew let down a rope by the ship's side

Up which she scrambled. Arethusa cried,

'Haul away!' The chain came up. The dolphins stood

Upon their tails. 'They'd make a crew,' said Hood,

'I'd sail with anywhere.' 'Goodbye,' Sadie called.

And now again the sails were all unfurled.

The seagulls danced beside them as the white wake curled

Till they were left behind. The ship sped on.

'Up to the crow's nest, child, and don't look down

Until you're safely there.' Hand over hand

Up the taut ratlines swiftly Sadie climbed

Till she was perched, shielding her eyes against the glare,

Above the glistening sea, and miles off, there

On the world's rim it seemed, a black shape sat

Right in their path, waiting like a cat

Beside a mousehole. 'A sail!' Sadie cried.

Afraid her small voice mightn't be heard

Clearly she scrambled down so fast her palms

Were stinging. 'The pirates,' Ajax said. Alarms

Were ringing throughout the ship, yet Sadie saw

No guns or swords or other signs of war.

N earer and nearer still their brave ship drew

To that black other crouching there until it grew

So big Sadie could see it clear and all its crew

Of villains. Just what was her surprise

To see that most of them were halfpint size.

'That one who wears a battered bowler hat,'

Said Ajax, 'Is their leader Captain Sprat.'

'But,' Sadie said, 'they must be dwarfs or gnomes.'

'That's right,' Ajax answered. 'Their small size comes

From working underground in bank vaults dark

Where they buy and sell and cheat and screech and bark

Like goblins.' 'But are there pirates then on shore?'

'More than on sea. Now hear their cannons roar.'

And so they did. The roundshot whistled overhead.

'They're after Arethusa,' Ajax said.

Sadie could see her standing proud and tall

And seeming not to mind the shot at all.

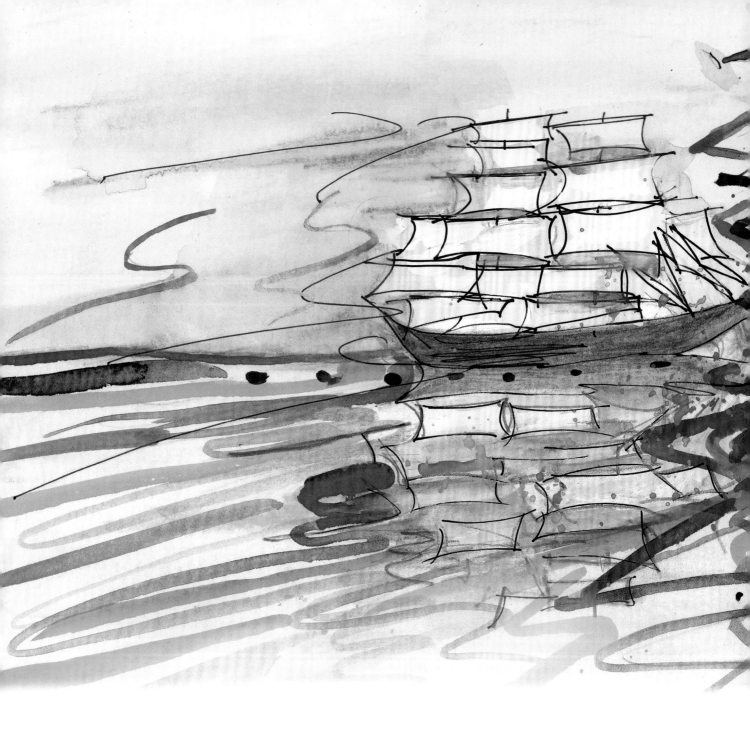

'Why don't we fire? They'll kill her.' 'No, you'll see.'
The Cutty Sark drove on relentlessly

Towards the pirate ship. 'We're going to ram.'

'Hold tight!' They struck her with a mighty slam.

The pirate ship had vanished. 'Where did it go?

Did it sink?' But Ajax shook his head. 'No.'

'They never sink. Like bubbles they go pop
    Whenever you face them squarely, top to top.
But run from them and they will hunt you down
And in their smothering broadside you can drown.'
'But will they come again?' 'Oh yes, indeed.
A chance to get their breath is all they need.'

'But not this trip.'

Day faded and the moon rose high.

They seemed to be sailing homeward through the sky.

'You see that spit ahead? That's Lizard Point.
We'll soon be there.' 'Oh. But I don't want...'
Sadie began. But already the coast
Was swimming on the larboard swiftly past
Until they turned and then began to run
Up the dark Thames, their voyage nearly done.

Sadie was torn in two. Though glad to be

Back home again, how she would miss the sea,

Ajax and Arethusa and the crew,

The tall, tall ship, the dolphins... 'Home for you,'

Said Arethusa, 'and never tell

What you saw once when you set sail

For treasure.' 'I won't,' said Sadie. 'Just one thing?'

The figureheads stood round her in a ring.

'Why do you need it?' 'Because we fear

We might be sold off and we like it here.'

They mentioned London Bridge, the Queen Mary too.

'It could be our turn next for all we know.

This treasure buys our stay. You wait and see

What happens. Now remember my words, and me.'

With Arethusa's voice still echoing in her head
She woke and couldn't remember how she got to bed

'Are you ready then?' her mother asked,

'To go to Auntie May's?' Sadie still basked

In an afterglow of dreams. 'Oh yes,' she said.

Her mother looked relieved. 'It'll do you good.'

She promised she'd come down too, when she could.

So Sadie took the train, happier because she'd been

To sea at last if only in a kind of dream.

But was it?

On the news one day she heard
Unknown benefactors had given a hoard
Of gold and jewels to the grateful nation
But that the gift had one condition:
Some of it must go to the Maritime Museum
To keep its treasures safe. Sadie smiled.
'What's that?' her aunt said. '*Once I sailed,*'
Sadie thought but held her tongue. She mustn't boast.
Perhaps one day she'd go again to a far coast!

One day again she'd be allowed to feel
The pluck of water underneath the keel.

'I thought I'd just go down the lane,' she said,
'And see the goat that lives outside the shed.'
She'd keep her secret safe inside his head.
Sadie sat down beside him on the grass.

'There was a ship,' she said.

'The smooth sea shone like glass...'

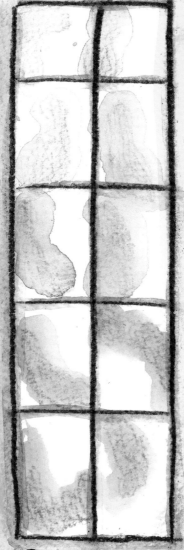

SHIP
FIGUREHEADS →

Ajax the Great

Characters

Ajax

In the Greek myths, Ajax was a courageous, giant warrior who fought in the Trojan War.

Arethusa

In the Greek myths she was a nymph whose Goddess, Artemis, transformed her into water so she could escape the God Alpheus. She became a stream of the clearest water, which is said to run under the sea to the island of Ortygia in Sicily.

Boadicea

She was the queen of the British Celtic Iceni tribe who led a fearless uprising against the occupying forces of the Roman Empire.

Hood

A famous admiral of Nelson's navy.

Glossary

Bosun: a ship's officer in charge of equipment and crew.

Broadside: the action of firing all the guns on one side of a navy ship at the same time.

Capstan: a machine used on ships for pulling heavy objects with a rope.

Crow's nest: lookout point at the top of the ship's sails.

Dry dock: an area that can be drained of water and used for repairing ships.

Ebb tide: the recurring movement of the sea away from the coast.

Figurehead: a wooden carving of a figure on the front of an old-fashioned sailing ship – they were seen as lucky charms, guiding the crew safely home through the oceans.

Galleon: comes from the Spanish word galeón, meaning armed merchant ship.

Grog: strong alcohol, often rum, that has been mixed with water.

Helen of Troy: her legendary beauty is said to have started the Trojan War.

The Isle of Dogs: a peninsula in London surrounded by the River Thames.

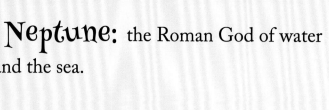

Keel: the underside of a ship or boat.

King Neptune: the Roman God of water and the sea.

Larboard: the left side of the ship.

Lizard Point: a southern tip of Cornwall and the starting point for many ocean voyages.

Log: an official record of events during the voyage of a ship.

London Bridge: sold to an American oil tycoon and shipped to Arizona where it was reassembled and stands today.

Pennants: a flag in the shape of a triangle.

Plymouth Sound: a bay in the English Channel.

Poop: deck.

The Queen Mary: a British ocean liner that was
sold to Long Beach, California where it remains in retirement.

Tortuga: a Caribbean island and pirate hot spot.

Ratlines: a series of small rope lines fastened
across a ship like the rungs of a ladder.

Round shot: ammunition in the form of
cast-iron or steel balls for firing from cannon.

Tricorne hat: a hat with the brim turned
up on three sides.

White wake: the waves or tracks in the sea left by a ship or boat.

Yardarm: a traditional nautical saying meaning
it is time for a morning drink.

Maureen Duffy was born in Sussex and is a poet, playwright, novelist and biographer. She has published forty books and sixteen plays. She is the President of the Authors Licensing and Copyright Society, and Vice President of the Royal Society of Literature. She is London President of the British Copyright Council, and a Fellow of King's College London. She was made a D.Litt. by Loughborough University and the University of Kent for services to literature and equality law. *Sadie and the Sea Dogs* is her first book for children. Duffy lives in London.

Anita Joice is a self-taught artist with a passion for children's book illustration. She has worked in academic publishing for many years and lived in Oxford, Beijing and North Carolina. She is a joyful artist who loves to create doorways to other worlds through paintings. She has a BA in Social Anthropology and Study of Religions (SOAS, London).